WORLDWIDE ADVENTURES 8

The Australian Boomerang
Bonanza

CATCH ALL OF FLAT STANLEY'S WORLDWIDE ADVENTURES:

AND DON'T MISS ANY OF THESE OUTRAGEOUS STORIES:

FLAT STANLEY's
WORLDWIDE ADVENTURES
BOOK No. 8

The Australian Boomerang Bonanza

CREATED BY **Jeff Brown**
WRITTEN BY **Josh Greenhut**
PICTURES BY **Macky Pamintuan**

SCHOLASTIC INC.
New York Toronto London Auckland
Sydney Mexico City New Delhi Hong Kong

ISBN 978-0-545-40277-4

12 11 10 9 8 7 6 5   12 13 14 15 16/0

Printed in the U.S.A.   40

First Scholastic printing, September 2011

Typography by Alison Klapthor

CONTENTS

The Grand Prize

Snow whipped through the air in thick blankets. Stanley Lambchop trudged on, trying not to flap in the wind.

Up ahead, Stanley could just make out his younger brother, Arthur. "Keep going!" Arthur's voice called. "We're almost there!"

Since the morning Stanley Lambchop had awakened to discover that he had been flattened by the bulletin board over his bed, he had traveled far and wide. He had trekked through the Mexican jungle. He had crossed the African savannah. He had braved the Canadian Arctic.

But this just might be his most difficult journey of all.

And it's only the walk home from school! thought Stanley.

He strained to take another step, but the wind blew him off his feet yet again. He flew backward into the side of a bus shelter with a slap.

Stanley groaned.

Since being flattened, Stanley could do all sorts of useful things. He could travel by mail, slide under doors, and fly like a kite. But being half an inch thick also had its disadvantages.

It sure doesn't help one bit in a blizzard! Stanley thought.

Arthur ran up. "Are you okay?" he cried over the howling wind.

Stanley gritted his chattering teeth. "I hate this weather!"

Arthur nodded and held out his hand. "Hold on to me!"

Stanley couldn't grab his brother's outstretched mitten. So Arthur leaned

into the wind and battled down the sidewalk, dragging Stanley's body flapping behind him like a cape.

"I wish we lived somewhere hot!" Stanley grumbled.

"Tell me about it!" Arthur called over his shoulder. "Can you believe that right now it's summer in Australia?!"

"We could be on a beach!" said Stanley.

"If only I'd won that Kanga Roos contest!" said Arthur. Kanga Roos was Arthur and Stanley's favorite breakfast cereal. Several months ago, Arthur had cut out a form from the back of their cereal box and entered a contest whose grand prize was a trip to Australia.

Nothing ever happened, though.

Arthur pulled Stanley up the front steps of their home. Pushing the door closed behind them, Stanley flattened himself against it and took a deep breath. A row of icicles fell from the side of his body.

"Thank you, Arthur," he said. "I don't know how I would have made it without you."

Arthur shrugged. "I don't know how you make it *anywhere* without me." He pulled off his boots. "After all, who was it that saved you on Mount Rushmore? Who solved all your problems over the telephone when you were in China? Who got us down that river in Africa?"

"You're the one who dropped the paddle!" cried Stanley, suddenly thawed under the collar.

"I did not!" replied Arthur. "*You dropped the paddle!*"

"I did not!" huffed Stanley.

"Arthur, is that you?" their mother's voice called from the next room.

Arthur held up his hands. "I'm just saying," he said in a low voice, "the next time you go somewhere, take me along, will you?" Then he added, "Especially if it's Hawaii or Florida."

Stanley couldn't help it. He smiled.

"You're here!" Mrs. Lambchop came bustling down the hall, her eyes fixed on Arthur. She seemed very excited.

"Wait until you—" The smile fell from her face. "Why, you look like a wet dog!"

Arthur scoffed. "I just walked through a blizzard!"

Their father, George Lambchop, appeared with a comb and started dragging it roughly through Arthur's hair.

"Dad!" protested Arthur.

Mrs. Lambchop bit her lip. "And his socks are all wet!"

Their parents didn't even seem to notice that Stanley's socks were wet, too.

"What is going on?" Arthur and Stanley both cried.

"There's someone important to see you, Arthur," Mr. Lambchop said in a strange voice. He stepped back to examine his handiwork and then wrinkled his nose.

"Just say you haven't had a chance to wash up," Mr. Lambchop whispered, and led the boys into the living room.

A barrel-chested man wearing a leather wide-brimmed hat was standing in the middle of the room. An official-looking young woman holding a clipboard stood behind him.

Arthur stopped in his tracks. "It's— But you're—" he sputtered.

Stanley stared at the man. He did look very familiar.

"G'day, Arthur," the man said in an accent that sounded . . . British? "Do you have something to say to me?"

Arthur looked at him blankly. "I haven't had a chance to wash up," he blurted.

The man's thick eyebrows danced up and down with amusement. Then, very mysteriously, he said: "Isn't there something else you should say, mate?"

Arthur gulped. He opened and shut his eyes. He swallowed. He pinched Stanley.

"Ouch!" Stanley cried.

"I'm not dreaming," Arthur croaked under his breath. Then, in a very loud, careful voice he began, "I JUST . . ."

Suddenly, Stanley knew exactly who the man was!

"JUMP...FOR...KANGA ROOS!" he and his brother shouted together, hopping up and down in time with the words, just like in the Kanga Roos commercials.

For the man standing before them was none other than Billy Wallaby, the Australian cereal magnate whose face graced the front of every box! This could mean only one thing:

"Looks like Arthur and a guest are coming with me to Australia!" Billy Wallaby announced.

The living room went wild. The woman with the clipboard clapped.

Arthur did a crazy dance. Harriet Lambchop started to cry. George Lambchop shook everybody's hand. Mr. Wallaby himself slapped Stanley on the back so hard that Stanley flipped over.

"I can't believe it!" said Arthur. "I never thought when I cut out that form from the back of the cereal box—"

"Never say never, mate," said Mr. Wallaby. "So, who are you going to take with you? Your mum or your dad?"

Stanley looked at the ground. He understood, of course. He had gone on so many trips without Arthur. It was only fair that Arthur got to have his own adventure for once.

And then Arthur did something that

surprised Stanley even more than an Australian billionaire showing up in their living room and giving away a trip to the other side of the world. He said, "Can Stanley come?"

The Aussie Crew

It had not been easy for Arthur to convince Mr. and Mrs. Lambchop to allow him and Stanley to travel to the other side of the globe without them. But the rules of the contest stated clearly that only two people could go, and Mr. Wallaby and his assistant, Ms. Perth, both promised that the boys would be carefully looked after.

Now, the Lambchop family stood on the tarmac in front of a small private jet, saying their good-byes as snow fell lightly around them.

Mrs. Lambchop hugged Stanley and Arthur tightly. Finally, Stanley whimpered, "Mom, you're going to wrinkle me."

"Of course," she said, letting them go and forcing a brave smile onto her face. "You know, there is a great deal of unusual slang in Australia, such as rhyming slang, where a rhyming word is used to signify another word. For instance, *dog and bone* means 'telephone,' and *plates of meat* means

'feet.' Isn't that fascinating? Did you know—"

"Mom," Arthur groaned.

"We'll be fine, Mom," Stanley said, more gently. He knew his mother was just rambling about the English language to make herself feel better. After all, it was her favorite subject.

Mr. Lambchop put a comforting arm around his wife. "Stanley," he said, "you are a more experienced traveler than your younger brother. We expect you to stay with him at all times."

Stanley saluted.

"Arthur," said Mr. Lambchop. "Keep the flat kid out of trouble."

Arthur cracked a smile.

Mr. Lambchop said nothing for a moment, and then he stepped forward and put one gloved hand on Arthur's shoulder and the other on Stanley's. Stanley could feel his father's hand resting near his cheek, like a warm blanket.

"Do you solemnly promise that you will take care of each other, no matter what?"

"We promise," Arthur and Stanley intoned.

Behind them, Ms. Perth had stepped out onto the top of the metal staircase that connected the plane to the tarmac.

"Time to go!" said Arthur. And before their parents could say another word, he grabbed Stanley's hand and sprinted for the plane.

"Bye, Mom! Bye, Dad!" called Stanley, his body once again flapping in the air behind his brother.

"Wow!" said Arthur, bouncing up and down. "Leather seats!"

"Arthur, Stanley, I'd like to introduce you to a few people," said Ms. Perth. An unshaven man wearing shorts, a T-shirt, and hiking boots ambled into the aisle. "This is Mr. Billabong, Mr. Wallaby's butler."

"You don't look like a butler," said Stanley.

Mr. Billabong grinned. "Yeah, well,

you don't look like a person, but you are, aren't ya? Call me Bongo!"

"And this," continued Ms. Perth, "is our chef, Sheila." She was an athletic-looking woman with curly red hair.

"How d'ya do, boys? Hope you like Vegemite!"

"What's Vegemite?" asked Arthur.

"I was hoping you'd say that!" cried Sheila, producing a plate from behind her back with two pieces of toast spread with a thin of layer of dark brown jam. "Try some!"

Arthur and Stanley each took a piece of toast. Exchanging looks, they took a bite.

Stanley stopped chewing at once. It

tasted like beef stew with old socks.

"Isn't it ace?!" said Sheila excitedly.

"That means 'great,'" Ms. Perth whispered.

"Oh, yes," said Arthur, his eyes watering as he forced himself to swallow.

"May we please have some water?" Stanley croaked.

"Two waters, coming right up!" said Bongo.

"Ready to see the pilot?" Ms. Perth asked.

She led them to the front of the plane and opened the door to the cockpit. The pilot turned to greet them, and Stanley

and Arthur gasped: It was Mr. Wallaby
himself!

"Take a seat, copilots," the billionaire
said, his eyebrows dancing. "Let's get
this boomerang in the air!"

Getting Down Under

High over the Pacific Ocean, Mr. Wallaby's voice filled the dim cockpit.

"The United States and Australia are like brothers, in my view," he said. "Almost exactly on opposite sides of the world, but we both have the same mum and dad, don't we? England. Then we traveled across oceans, made our own destinies. Americans and Australians, we're explorers and adventurers. Our countries are almost the same size. Did you know that? Excluding Hawaii and Alaska, of course. You boys and me, we have a lot in common."

The last six hours had flown by. Stanley, Arthur, and Mr. Wallaby had spent the entire time swapping stories of adventure. Mr. Wallaby had climbed Mount Everest and jumped off the tallest building in Asia. He had driven race cars and sailed around the world. He had been poor as a child, and then he made himself into one of the richest men in Australia.

Arthur sighed. "I wish I could do everything well, like you," he said.

Mr. Wallaby shook his head. "No, mate, you got it wrong. It's the people who think they can do everything that get into trouble. What's most important is to face up to what you *can't* do, and make up for that. I learned that the hard way."

"What do you mean?" asked Arthur.

"Take Stanley here," said Mr. Wallaby. "He's flat. What's he have to worry about?"

Arthur thought. "Getting sat on?"

"The ends of escalators?" guessed Stanley.

"No!" shouted Mr. Wallaby. "The wind! The wind is your greatest adversary, mate! You were blown off

Mount Rushmore, blown halfway across Canada, thrown from the Great Wall of China! You can barely make it home from school on a windy day! If I were you, I'd worry about the wind, mate. That's the greatest threat to your well-being."

Stanley nodded. He'd never thought about it that way before. "So what do you have to worry about, Mr. Wallaby?"

"Me?" The man's bushy eyebrows collapsed, and he sighed. "Ask Ms. Perth, she'll tell you. I lose things. Computers, wallets, watches, papers. If I were a kangaroo, I'd lose my pouch. Lost my own brother in the bush once. Still looking for him, actually."

Stanley was about to ask Mr. Wallaby to explain when Arthur said, "And me?"

"You?" said Mr. Wallaby. He studied Arthur carefully, and then his eyebrows rose like the sun. "Cheeseburgers. Your stomach's growling louder than my jet engines! Bongo! Sheila!"

Torches lit the beach and music filled the air. Hundreds of people danced in the sand. Arthur and Stanley leaned back against the bamboo counter, sipping their ginger ales.

Bongo sauntered up beside them. "Quite a party you're having, Mr. Lambchop!"

Arthur grinned. "Thanks, Bongo."

"What do you say, boys," called Sheila from behind the counter. "Should I throw some more prawns on the barbie?"

Arthur leaned close to Stanley. "Maybe this is that rhyming slang Mom told us about," he said under his breath.

"Prawn means shrimp!" Bongo boomed between them. "And *barbie* is barbecue to you! That last bit rhymed, didn't it?"

"Oh, grilled shrimp!" said Arthur. "Sure, Sheila!"

"Thanks, Sheila," Stanley chimed in. "All the food's delicious!"

"No worries!" said Sheila.

Two girls came up to them, giggling.

"Are you Arthur Lambchop, the boy who won the contest?" said the one with long blonde hair.

Arthur gulped. "Yes," he said.

"Congratulations!" said the girl. "I'm Mimi, and this is my sister, Juli. We read about you in the newspaper!"

Juli leaned close to Stanley. "Is it true that you were flattened by a bulletin board?" Her eyes were wide and crystal

blue like the ocean.

All Stanley could think to say was, "Uh huh."

"We're going to dance," said Mimi.

"You should come!" said Juli.

Stanley and Arthur tried to resist, but Juli and Mimi wouldn't take no for an answer. Soon, they were out in the sand, dancing and singing along with everyone else. Then Mr. Wallaby took the microphone and said, "To our grand prize winner, Arthur Lambchop, and to his brother, Stanley! To fate and the spirit of adventure! To Australia!" The crowd's cheers were louder than the sound of crashing waves. The next thing Stanley knew, both he and his brother had been hoisted into the air and were being passed over people's heads in time with the music.

Stanley looked up at the stars twinkling down on his flat body as he surfed atop the crowd. He twisted his head and caught Arthur's eye.

"Best trip ever!" screamed Arthur.

Stanley couldn't agree more.

An Almost Perfect Day

The next morning, Bongo and Sheila took the boys surfing. The breaking waves slapped into Stanley's flat legs as they waded into the ocean. "Have either of you ever surfed before?" asked Sheila.

Arthur and Stanley both shook their heads.

"Stan here could be a surfboard all by himself!" Bongo said, laughing.

"Hey, that's a good idea," said Arthur seriously. "Maybe I could surf on Stanley."

"I think I'd sink with you on my back," Stanley said apologetically.

Sheila looked Stanley up and down, and then looked at the very end of her surfboard. "He doesn't have to stand on your back. He can balance on the bottoms of your feet!"

She threw her belly on her surfboard and started paddling.

"Bongo, put the boys on your board. Let's go catch some big ones!"

* * *

"Here it comes!" said Arthur. "Ready?"
Stanley floated on the surface. He
twisted his head around to find a wall
of water rising behind them like a
skyscraper.

The giant wave thrust them forward
like a shot, with Arthur balancing on
the bottoms of Stanley's feet. Stanley
felt Arthur make a tiny movement,
and Stanley's body swung alongside
the wave. Arthur twitched again, and
Stanley's body swung around the other
way.

They were surfing!

Before Stanley's eyes, the wave
curled around them. Stanley could
see blue sky at the end of the tunnel

of water, and Arthur leaned forward. Stanley raced on, the tunnel getting smaller and smaller, until they burst through a curtain of white foam into calmer water.

"Awesome!" Arthur and Stanley shouted together. Arthur leaped off.

"Good on ya!" cried Bongo.

"Ace!" screamed Sheila.

On the shore, Stanley could see Ms. Perth and Mr. Wallaby pumping their arms in the air.

That afternoon, they went snorkeling on Mr. Wallaby's yacht.

Stanley adjusted his face mask and snorkel and wiggled each of his feet to make sure his flippers were on tight. He gave Bongo the thumbs-up and jumped off the back of the yacht, following Arthur into the water.

"There's nothing like the Great Barrier Reef," Mr. Wallaby had told them. "It's an underwater kingdom of coral—alive, every bit of it. You've been to the Great Wall of China, Stanley. Some people think that's visible from space, but they're wrong. The reef is the only structure made by living things that's grand enough for *that*."

A giant green sea turtle swam before Stanley's eyes. A school of clownfish, with their neon orange and white stripes, darted below.

Stanley pumped his flippers lightly and burst forward through the water. Suddenly, he realized that with his flat shape and his flippers, he could move very quickly. He looked around for Arthur and spotted him in the distance. It took only a few quick pumps of Stanley's flippers to get to him.

Stanley held out his hand to Arthur and gestured for him to take it.

With a kick of his flippers, Stanley pulled Arthur along behind him, just as Arthur had done for him so many times before. Together, they darted smoothly, effortlessly, just below the surface of the water. Bright coral in a thousand different colors lit the way.

Suddenly, Arthur squeezed Stanley's hand and gestured to their left. There was a pair of dolphins swimming right next to them!

Stanley reached over with his free hand and pinched his brother.

Arthur glared as if to say, what did you do that for?

Stanley raised his eyebrows, and Arthur's sudden smile made it clear he understood. Stanley was doing the same thing Arthur had done to him when they'd discovered Mr. Wallaby in their living room.

We're not dreaming, they both thought.

* * *

Walking on the beach, Arthur and Stanley watched a man throwing a boomerang. It would arc high into the air and then swing back and land smoothly in his hand. Over and over again, like a graceful bird against the setting sun, the boomerang would sail away and then return. Sometimes, the wind would change the boomerang's course, and the man would have to run a few steps to catch it.

The wind ruffled Arthur's hair. "I bet you could do that," he said to Stanley.

Stanley tilted his head matter-of-factly. "I bet I could."

Stanley lay on his side on the ground,

and Arthur took hold of one foot and one arm.

"Bend your body," Arthur instructed.

"I was a Flying Chinese Wonder, remember?" joked Stanley.

In the distance, Stanley heard someone call his name.

"Here goes nothing," said Arthur. He spun around, holding on to Stanley,

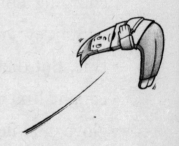

faster and faster, like a shot putter. Stanley thought he saw a group of people running along the beach, and then Arthur heaved him into the air.

"Stanley, Arthur, no!" Mr. Wallaby's voice exploded across the sand. "THE WIND!"

Stanley now saw that it was Mr. Wallaby, Ms. Perth, Bongo, and Sheila charging along the shoreline.

Stanley was about to yell that he was fine. But then a powerful gust of wind caught him in the back like a boxing glove, and he lost his bent shape. And, all at once, the wind whisked him away from the ocean.

"STANLEY!" Arthur's voice called.

"ARTHUR!" Stanley screamed.

But he was already too far away. Stanley could just make out a cluster of people jumping up and down in the sand before he flew out of sight.

To the Back
of Beyond

A mountain range loomed below. Stanley tried to point himself downward for an emergency landing, but the wind rolled him over and over. It was no use. He couldn't get down.

And then Stanley heard a rumbling in the distance. He scanned the horizon Storm clouds straight ahead! A bundle of dark clouds flashed in warning. What if I get hit by lightning? Stanley thought.

Again, he tried desperately to make himself descend. He held his hands and feet in front of him, and folded himself in half lengthwise. He twisted his body into a spiral. But the wind just grew more powerful. It was pushing him right into the storm.

Stanley felt a drop of rain on the back of his neck, then another. Soon he felt like he was being pelted from all sides. His body flapped like an untied sail. Stanley thought of Arthur, pulling him through the blizzard to safety.

But Arthur was still back on the beach, alone.

I was supposed to take care of him, thought Stanley. I made a solemn promise to stay with my little brother . . . and I broke it.

He imagined Arthur crying.

A drop fell from the flat of Stanley's cheek, and he didn't know if it was rain. He buried his face in his hands. He flinched every time the thunder clapped. Then, slowly, the air currents started to lift him higher. He peeked out from between his fingers. Gray clouds were flying by his face.

Suddenly, Stanley emerged into a brilliant red sky. He was above the storm. The dark clouds were rumbling wildly beneath him, like a flashing, lumpy blanket, but he knew he was safe, at least for the moment.

Stanley looked at the sky all around him. It was as bright as the coral in the Great Barrier Reef.

Don't worry, Arthur, Stanley thought bravely. You're not alone. I'll be back as soon as I can.

Late the next day, Stanley fluttered down to earth at last. He got to his feet and peered around. Red soil and low, dry bushes stretched toward the horizon.

The outback, Stanley realized. Stanley had learned at school that Australia was the only continent that was an island,

and he remembered what Mr. Wallaby had said, about how it was similar in size to the United States of America. The outback was the vast, arid region in the middle.

It's going to be a long walk back to the beach, Stanley thought. His stomach grumbled loudly.

The sun sets in the west, he remembered, and the Great Barrier Reef is on the east coast.

With a sigh, he turned his back on the setting sun and started on his way.

Soon, Stanley came across a group of kangaroos. Several of them had joeys in their pouches. Two big kangaroos were hopping up and down and hitting each other playfully.

I didn't know kangaroos really boxed! thought Stanley, creeping closer. One of them landed a stiff right jab.

"Ooh!" Stanley cried.

All of the kangaroos turned to look at him. And then, as if on cue, they hopped away.

"Wait!" cried Stanley, stumbling after them. He saw how the kangaroos pushed off with their hind legs and sprang through the air.

Without thinking, Stanley bent his feet beneath him, arched his back, and pushed off of his shins. He sprang a few feet forward, landed, and then pushed off again.

I can hop! Stanley realized. With his bendable shape, he could spring through the air. Not only that, he could hop much faster than he could walk or run!

Stanley hopped after the kangaroos, the ground springing away and then rising up to meet his legs, until the sky had turned from red to dark blue. Finally, the animals came to rest in a sparse wood. Stanley sank to his knees, panting.

Stanley noticed a kangaroo with a joey in her pouch eyeing him, and suddenly she hopped over. He got to his feet slowly.

"Hi," Stanley said politely. The joey and its mother stared at him.

"Thanks for letting me follow you," he continued.

Without thinking, Stanley made a playful jab, and the mother kangaroo blinked and bobbed her head. Then she hopped forward and punched Stanley in his empty stomach.

Stanley fell to the ground with a groan. Above him, the joey seemed to smile, and then disappeared as the mother hopped off.

Stanley saw stars, but they may have been in the sky. In his head, he heard someone laughing at him.

Then he realized it wasn't in his head. The laughter was coming from nearby, where he could just make out a campfire flickering among the trees.

The Bush Tracker

Stanley crept forward through the bush. There was a man squatting by the fire, humming lightly to himself. His clothes were dirty, and his hands were black. His skin was leathery. Someone laughed nearby.

Stanley craned his neck, trying to see who else was around.

"You want me to sing it again, do

ya?" the man said. "Don't suppose you want 'Waltzing Matilda,' instead?"

Again, the other voice laughed heartily.

The man chuckled to himself. Then a low, tender voice erupted from his throat. He sang,

"Kookaburra sits in the old gum tree

Merry, merry king of the bush is he

Laugh, Kookaburra, laugh, Kookaburra!

Gay your life must be."

A bird fluttered into view and landed right on the man's shoulder. Without turning his head, the man held up a hand, and the bird pecked some seeds from between his fingers.

And then the bird let out a laugh!

It's a real kookaburra! marveled Stanley. He took a step forward, and a dry twig snapped underfoot.

The bird disappeared from the man's shoulder, and he stopped singing. He scanned the trees. Then he stood up and took a few slow steps right toward Stanley.

"I can tell from the sound of that twig that you're no kangaroo," the man said, narrowing his eyes. "And you're no dingo, either. I'd almost say you were a person, except . . ."

Stanley stepped into the clearing.

The man raised his big eyebrows.

"Except you're flatter than a platypus's bill." He chuckled warmly to himself. "Didn't expect that, did I?" He returned to his place by the fire. The kookaburra fluttered back onto his shoulder.

"So what's a thin joey like you doing spying on old Wally?" the man said without looking up.

"I'm lost," Stanley admitted.

"I should say you are," said the man. "All the way out here at the back of beyond. It's not called the Never Never for nothing. You're awful deep in the bush, mate. What'd you do, get blown away by a strong wind?" the man joked.

The kookaburra laughed.

When Stanley didn't answer, the man looked up, and his eyebrows made a tent. "That's really what happened, isn't it?"

Stanley nodded, and then he couldn't help it. His flat cheeks were suddenly wet.

"I left my little brother on the beach by the Great Barrier Reef," he said.

"The Great Barrier Reef!" the man exclaimed. "That's more than one thousand miles away!"

Stanley's whole body shook.

The man stood up. "No worries, joey," he said. "I know what it's like to be apart from your family. Old Wally is going to get you back where you belong." He patted Stanley awkwardly on the back.

"You must be starving," Wally said quickly. "Come on. Let's get you some grubs."

"Thank you," Stanley sniffled. "Grub sounds great."

"Have more than one, mate," Wally said, chuckling. He opened his fist, which was full of tiny white worms.

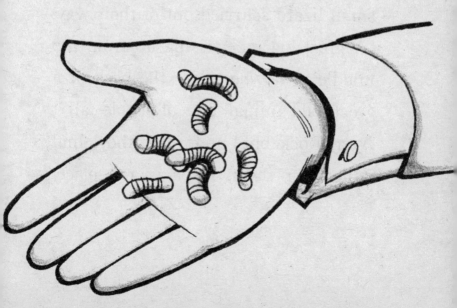

"The trick is to get 'em before they squirm away!"

They set out at dawn the next morning. Wally said they were a two-day trek from the nearest ranger station, near Uluru.

"Uluru?" said Stanley.

"The most majestic place on the planet, if you ask me," said Wally, as a small lizard scurried out of their way. "A great big rock, rising up from the middle of nowhere like the back of a great wild animal. Lots of people call it Ayers Rock, but I prefer the Aboriginal name. For them, it's a sacred place.

They say Uluru was built up by two boys playing in the mud during creation times. Brothers, maybe."

Stanley thought of Arthur with a pang. "Do you have any brothers or sisters?" he asked.

Wally shrugged. "Dunno," he said. "I'm an orphan. A bush tracker found me by a watering hole when I was just a tyke. Must have—"

Wally froze and held up a dirty hand in front of Stanley.

Through the sparse trees, Stanley saw a horse, munching on dry bush.

"A brumby," Wally whispered. He crept forward.

"A what?" said Stanley.

Wally's eyebrows crouched together. "A wild horse. Catch him, and we could cut two days off the trip, easy."

"I guess this means you're either going to roll me or sit on me," muttered Stanley, remembering his trip to Mount Rushmore.

Wally looked at him sideways. "I wouldn't do a thing like that," he said. He bent to the ground, picked up a short, thick stick, and handed it to Stanley. "Can't tame a horse without reins, can I?"

"But that horse doesn't have reins," said Stanley, confused.

Wally showed Stanley how to grip

each end of the stick. Then he wiggled
his eyebrows and said, "Now he does."

With that, Wally grabbed Stanley
and leaped for the horse.

Uluru

The brumby raced across the landscape. Stanley's belly rested on its neck, while his arms stretched forward on either side so the horse could bite the stick between his hands. Meanwhile, Wally held both of Stanley's legs as he rode the brumby's bare back.

At first, both Stanley and the horse had been terrified. But Wally had reacted in his calm, amused away, joking with Stanley and the horse until they'd both relaxed. Now, Stanley had begun to enjoy himself. They were going so fast!

A pair of emu ran for a moment beside them, and then were left behind.

If only Arthur could see this! Stanley thought. He gave a whoop as the world whipped by, and Wally chuckled behind him.

After a few hours, they dismounted, and Wally led Stanley and the brumby on a walk through the bush to look for lunch. As they walked, Wally sang "Waltzing Matilda" in his low, sweet voice: "Waltzing Matilda, waltzing Matilda, you'll come a-waltzing Matilda with me."

"Might as well be the Australian national anthem, that one," he told Stanley. He pointed out animal tracks as they went. Wally could tell what sort of animal made a track, whether it was a boy or a girl, even how old it was—all from how big and deep the track was. At one point, he kneeled down and drew Stanley's attention to an impression in the dust.

"Tiger snake," murmured Wally. "Heading that way, fast. He's a poisonous devil, he is."

Soon, they were back on the

brumby's back. As the afternoon wore on, Stanley's body ached, and he was covered in dust. Then, just as the sun was dropping to the horizon, Wally tugged Stanley's legs, bringing the brumby to a sudden stop.

"There she is," said Wally softly.

Stanley craned his neck to look up. In the distance, rising from the flat, barren outback, was a wide, smooth red rock.

It was much bigger than Stanley expected.

Wally kicked the horse with his heels, and they took off at a gallop.

Soon, Uluru towered before them, glowing a bright purplish red in the

setting sun. It almost looked as if it were lit from within.

I see why this is a sacred place, thought Stanley.

Suddenly, Stanley saw a swirl of dust heading for them. It was a Jeep. As it got closer, Stanley saw heads sticking out the windows and one out the top. The one from the roof was waving its arms wildly, bobbing up and down.

And then Stanley's heart lurched.

It was Arthur.

"Wally, it's him!" Stanley screamed. "It's him!"

As soon as the brumby stopped, Stanley leaped to the ground and sprinted for the Jeep.

He could hear Arthur's voice now, high in the air. "Stanley! Stanley!"

The Jeep skidded to a stop, and everyone poured out. Mr. Wallaby, Ms. Perth, Bongo, and Sheila raced toward Stanley—but Arthur overtook them all and barreled into him, wrapping himself in Stanley's flat body like a blanket.

"I'm really sorry, Stanley," said Arthur. "I promised to stay with you, and I sent you flying halfway across Australia."

"I'm the one who should be sorry," said Stanley. "I left my little brother all alone on a beach. What would Mom say?"

Arthur thought for a second. "Probably something about grammar."

Stanley grinned. "How'd you find me?"

Mr. Wallaby stepped forward. "We've been tracking you by satellite photo since yesterday. We just didn't want to come rescue you in a helicopter, because we feared you'd blow aw—" Mr. Wallaby's eyebrows twitched, and he abruptly stopped talking.

He was looking straight at Wally.

Wally shifted uncomfortably. "G'day," said Wally. "I'm Wally."

Mr. Wallaby walked slowly up to the bush tracker, and Stanley suddenly realized that Mr. Wallaby's lip was quivering. "I know who you are."

He threw his arms around Wally, and Wally flinched.

"You're my brother," declared Mr. Wallaby. Ms. Perth, Bongo, and Sheila all gasped. The two men studied each other's faces. Wally was leaner and darker from the sun, but Stanley had to admit that they had the same eyebrows. "Mum and Dad were trekking through the outback with us. You and I were playing by a watering hole. And then I . . . I lost you."

Wally swallowed, and his eyebrows rose and then fell. After a moment, he said, "What's your name, then?"

"Billy," answered Mr. Wallaby.

Wally chuckled to himself. "That does sound familiar."

Billy and Wally Wallaby hugged again, and so did Arthur and Stanley Lambchop, as Ms. Perth, Bongo, and Sheila wiped their eyes. Uluru glowed warmly above them all.

Together Again

Standing in front of the Sydney Opera House, Mr. Wallaby had his arms around Stanley and Arthur as he addressed the crowd. The magnificent building rose up behind them like a collection of giant sails.

"Today is about much more than a contest on the back of a cereal box," he said into the microphone. "It's about

the bond of brotherhood that unites us all, as nations and as people. It is about finding what once was lost, and treasuring it all the more. I'll never forget what these young boys have taught me. They showed me what being a good brother is all about! Ladies and gentlemen, I would like to introduce my own long-lost brother, Wally Wallaby!"

Cameras flashed as Wally stepped up and laid a hand on Stanley's shoulder. The crowd burst into applause. Off to the side, Bongo whistled loudly as Ms. Perth wiped her eyes. "Ace!" cried Sheila.

"Beyond that, I have only one thing

to say," said Mr. Wallaby. His eyes twinkled and his eyebrows wiggled. "I . . . JUST . . ."

Arthur, Stanley, and the hundreds of people around them jumped up and down. "JUMP . . . FOR . . . KANGA ROOS!"

Back at home, around the breakfast table, Stanley and Arthur stuffed Kanga Roos cereal into their mouths as fast as they could.

"Can we be excused?" Arthur and Stanley said together.

Mr. Lambchop nodded from behind his newspaper, and they darted out of

the kitchen and down the hall to their bedroom. On the bulletin board over Stanley's bed hung a boomerang, which Wally and Mr. Wallaby had given them the day they left Australia. They'd both signed it: "To Arthur and Stanley, Our Long-Lost Brothers. Yours, Wally & Billy."

"So kangaroos really can box?" said Arthur, jumping up and down on his bed.

"Uh huh," said Stanley, folding his feet beneath him, resting on his shins, and springing up and down.

Arthur hopped down to the ground, and for a moment they bounced in front of each other, grinning wildly and brandishing their fists.

They both threw a jab. And just like that, another round began.

WHAT YOU NEED TO KNOW BEFORE YOUR OWN ADVENTURE DOWN UNDER

The name Australia comes from the Latin *Terra Australis Incognito*, which means the *Unknown Southern Land*.

Australia has an average of three people per square kilometer. It has one of the lowest population densities in the world.

Sheep outnumber people in Australia by almost eight to one: there are 150 million sheep and only 20 million people!

Australia is the only continent on Earth occupied by only one nation. It is also the lowest and flattest continent.

The Great Barrier Reef is more than 2,000 km long (bigger than England!) and is the largest organic construction on Earth. It is the only living thing that astronauts in the International Space Station can see from space without a telescope.

The Great Barrier Reef has a mailbox! You can take a ferry out there and send a postcard from it, stamped with the Great Barrier Reef stamp.

The "Surf Lifesavers"—surfers who act as lifeguards—originated in Australia over a hundred years ago. They have since spread to many other countries.

Australian English has plenty of its own slang, including "clobber" (clothes), "mozzies" (mosquitos), and "ripper" (terrific). Go on, give it a burl! (That means, give it a try!)